The Monster Hunt

Cynthia Rider • Alex Brychta

OXFORD
UNIVERSITY PRESS

Gran took the children on
a monster hunt.

Biff saw some monster footprints.

Chip saw a monster glove,
and . . .

Kipper saw the monster!

"Come on," said Gran.
"Let's get that monster!"

The monster ran.
It ran up the hill.

It ran into the mill . . .
and hid.

"Come on," said Chip.
"Let's get that monster!"

They went into the mill.

"Ssh!" said Gran.

"I can see the monster's tail."

Gran pulled the monster's tail.
"Got you!" she said.

"AARGH!" said the monster.

Crash! went a sack.

Crash! went the monster.

The monster looked at
the children.
"Help!" he said.

"Monsters!"

Think about the story

Why do you think Gran and the children went on a monster hunt?

How did the children know which way the monster had gone?

How would you feel if you got covered in flour?

Would you like to go on a monster hunt? What would you do if you caught the monster?

Matching

Match the monster to its shadow.